DAY IN SEPTEMBER

CREATIVE

EDITIONS

HARCOURT

BRACE &

COMPANY

Designed by Rita Marshall

DAY IN SEPTEMBER

BY

YAN NASCIMBENE

The tour boat glides along the quays, its flood-lights projecting ghostly shadows on the ceiling and walls of Raphaël's bedroom. **RAPHAËL** lies awake; he cannot sleep. He is alone tonight. Every night he is alone. He looks at the moving shadows, thinking of the tour boat full of cheerful sightseers, drifting down the river. The rumble of its engine fades away, and so too the laughter and conversations in mysterious, foreign tongues. The bedroom once again is plunged into darkness.

Raphaël's father and mother are out. They might be at the opera, at the cinema, in some noisy and elegant restaurant, at a friend's home. Perhaps they are walking along the river, crossing a bridge, looking down at the brightly lit tour boat. They might be on the boat itself, laughing amid the tourists. Or maybe they are hidden away in a secret place. Raphaël wonders. His thoughts comfort him against the silence of his bedroom, the silence of the numerous rooms in the apartment, the stillness of each object around him. His scattered toys and pencils, his pants and shirt folded on the chair, every box, every painting, the statue on the mantle, the vases, every piece of furniture, the arches and columns—everything is dark and lifeless.

4

DAY

IN

SEP

TEM

BER

7

Paris is large and busy. Every night, every day, Raphaël's parents are out: shopping, working, always rushing. Unlike his parents, Raphaël does not know the city very well. He knows the way to school and back. He seldom goes out.

Another tour boat passes in the night. Again the shadows of branches and leaves and of the wrought-iron balcony move across the room, softly caressing every object in it. They run over his bed, over his body and once again fade away.

∽∽∽∽∽

As Raphaël finally falls asleep, **ESTELLA**, half a world away, gathers her books. Soon the bell will ring and school will be over.

Leaving town, the school bus gradually empties. Fields of vegetables replace the last few scattered houses. Bare land replaces the fields. When the bus reaches Cactus Corners, Estella is the only child left. She gets off and it turns around. The engine roars as the driver shifts gears. Then the bus fades away, back to the suburbs and the downtown school. The wind is hot. A thin coat of dust covers the road sign, the prickly pears, the run-down café. Estella walks along the dirt road all the way to

Maxwell Ranch. This is where she lives, on the edge of the Mojave Desert in California.

Maxwell Ranch isn't a ranch anymore. There are no cattle; nothing grows but a few dry shrubs. Clouds of powdery dust swirl between the water tank, the landlord's house and the chicken coop. There are no chickens, either. The chicken coop had been abandoned long ago. Mr. Maxwell, the landlord, now rents it to Estella's parents, who have fixed it into a small home.

After doing her homework Estella plays outside. She plays alone in the smooth, dry dirt. With a stick she draws pictures in the sand: dragons and monsters, birds and snakes. Stacking stones, she builds a castle. The faint noise of an engine colors the silence. Estella listens, motionless, her hands in midair. First like the humming of an insect, it becomes closer, more precise. She stands up and looks in the distance. The rumble intensifies. Soon she sees the round cloud of dust, then the truck itself, still just a dot. Now the truck approaches. It passes by without slowing down and vanishes far away, along the straight endless road.

彡彡彡彡彡

DAY

IN

SEP

TEM

BER

Early in the morning **RAPHAËL** is awakened by the garbage and delivery trucks. A few cars follow, then more cars until it becomes one constant noisy flow of throbbing engines and impatient horns. That is when Mademoiselle Rosamère turns on the light in Raphaël's bedroom and tells him to get up.

Mademoiselle Rosamère takes care of Raphaël. She helps him get dressed. She eats with him the breakfast that the cook has prepared. She takes him to school. She picks him up after school. She puts him to bed. Mademoiselle Rosamère also has to help the maid with cleaning, shopping and answering the phone. She is very busy. She says so constantly: "I don't have time! I am very busy!" Although Raphaël's parents never say so, they too are busy. Either they are out being busy, or at the opposite end of the apartment, many rooms away, in the library or in their bedroom, always busy.

Lying on his back, Raphaël counts the stucco wreaths of leaves that hang around the high ceiling of his bedroom. He has counted them many times. The front door opens and closes. Raphaël recognizes the peculiar clicking sound of the lock. He hears the footsteps. He can easily identify them:

Y A N • N A S

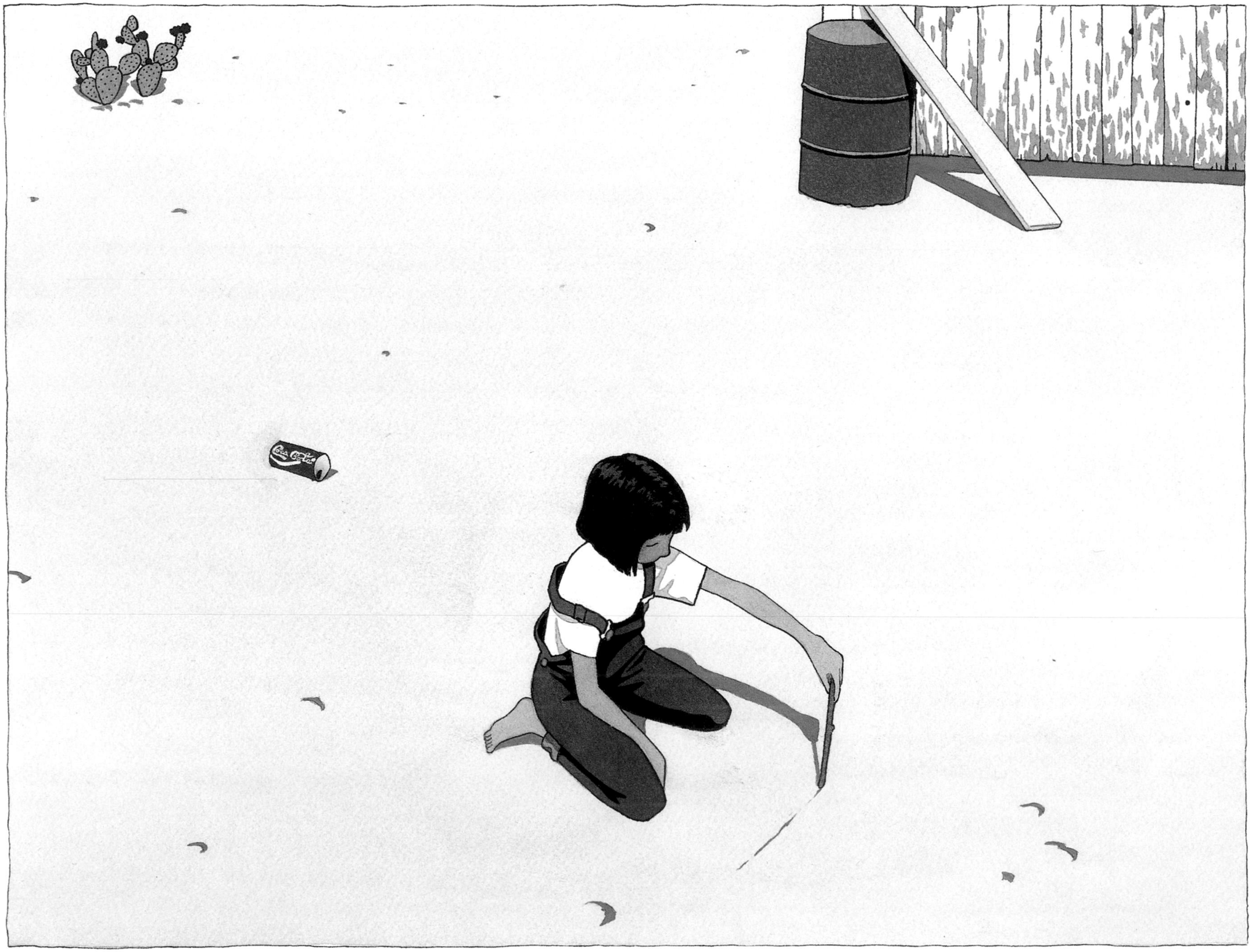

his mother's, his father's, Mademoiselle Rosamère's, the maid's, the cook's. They come and go. Sometimes they seem to get closer. Raphaël listens. Then they fade away.

Raphaël listens to the silence. The floor creaks. The wind rustles the leaves outside his window. There is the distant clinking of glasses and plates, voices from the kitchen and the street, a dog barking, the muffled hum of the elevator. It stops. Raphaël holds his breath. The elevator starts again. He listens to his own breathing, slow and regular. The silence whispers a warm and soothing lullaby.

≈≈≈≈

Aside from the creaking sound of Mr. Maxwell's screen door and the occasional passage of a truck, the silence weighs undisturbed across the Mojave Desert, from the distant purple range to Estella's sand pictures and castle. The constant buzzing of flies does not taint the silence but rather belongs to it. It is the music of heat. **ESTELLA** sits on the ground, her bare arms and feet covered with white dust. The blue shadow of the chicken coop creeps toward her, reaches her, swallows her and moves on. It stretches across the road before the old

11

pickup truck finally comes to a stop.

Every day Estella listens to the truck as it gets closer and closer. She recognizes its sound but ignores it through fear of making it vanish. Hearing the grinding of the brakes and the two doors being slammed, she smiles. Still she doesn't look up. Her mother and father call her. Finally she jumps to her feet, runs toward them, embraces them. They hug each other, all three clinging to one another for an instant. A very short instant. Much remains to be done; dinner is to be prepared, clothes to be washed and hung to dry, an oil leak in the truck to be fixed. Estella's parents ask her to translate into Spanish a letter from the Sun Tomato Farm Company. They would like to ask Estella about school, tell each other stories—anything to forget about the tomatoes they picked all day, crates full of tomatoes, mounds and mountains of tomatoes. But soon after dinner they fall asleep, fully dressed. Tomorrow morning, before dawn, before Estella will awaken, they will leave for another day's work.

Estella slips snugly between them. She likes the warmth of their bodies. While looking through the open window at the stars, she gently strokes their calloused hands.

After school, just like Estella, **RAPHAËL** does his homework. For the most part, he doesn't do it with much interest, but he does enjoy history and geography. They allow him to travel to distant places and distant times. He discovers new, unexplored countries, tames wild and exotic animals, fishes with polar bears and kingfishers, hunts with grizzly bears and tigers. He climbs high mountains, paddles a canoe across a dark lake, crawls through thick forests smelling of ferns and moss. He sails on a frigate to far-away islands. He chases pirates, sinks their vessels. He fights barbarians. He rides through the desert . . .

"Have you finished your homework? Raphaël! Are you listening? And please sit up straight!"

Mademoiselle Rosamère's unexpected shriek has made Raphaël fall off his horse. He nods and smiles politely, but as she rushes out of the room, he closes his eyes and jumps back in the saddle.

His stallion, the fastest in the West, leaves a trail of dust as it gallops across the vast open land. He rides through a canyon, up and down steep slopes, through the immensity of the desert. He has

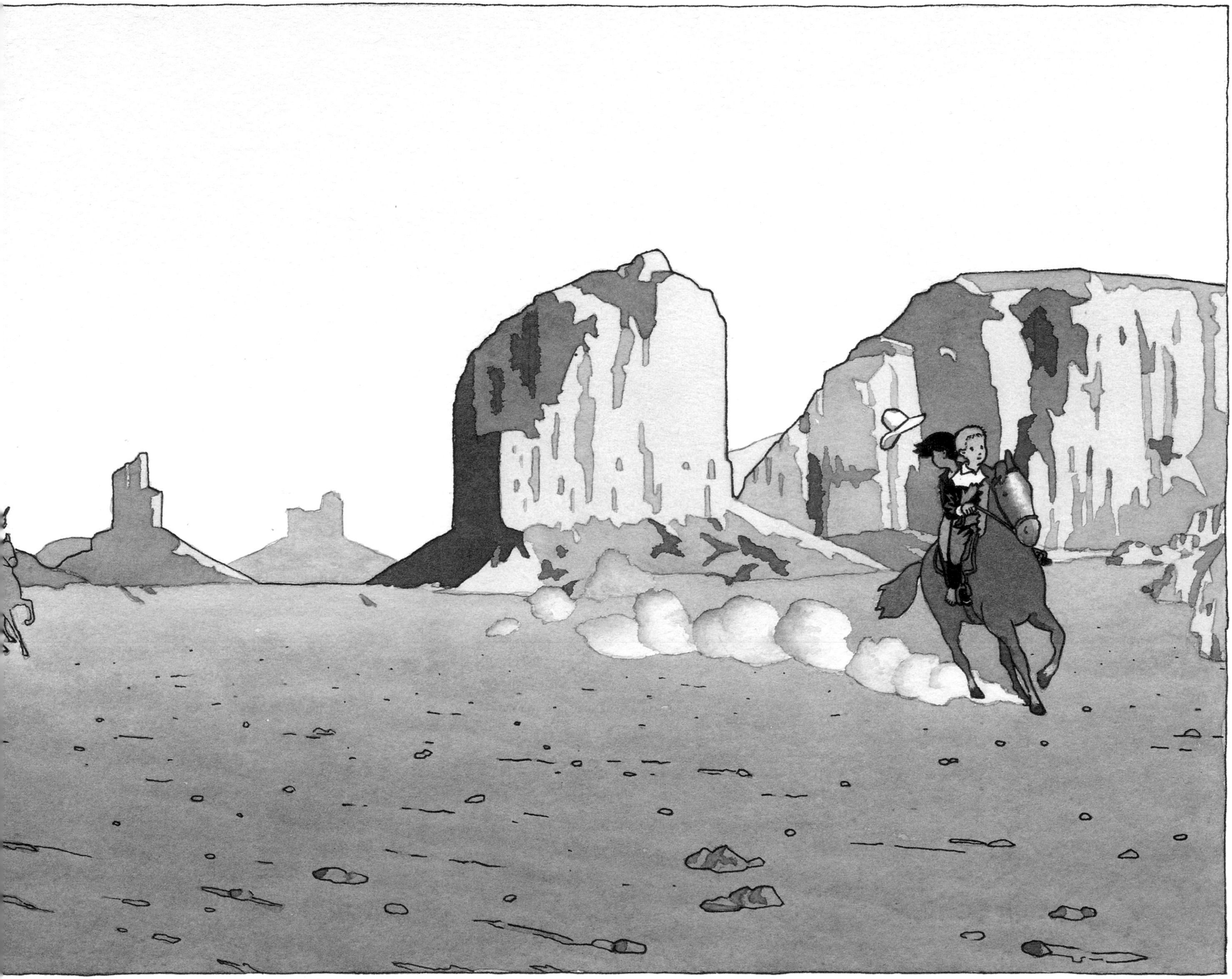

been riding night and day. Now the outlaws are in sight. Two, three, four, five! Five and a prisoner tied up across the leader's saddle. Raphaël is catching up. They pull out their guns, they shoot, he ducks. Raphaël and the leader (who looks like Raphaël's math teacher) are galloping side by side, full speed, past cactus, across a creek, jumping over huge boulders. Raphaël leans toward the leader, pushes him off his horse, grabs the prisoner. As they escape from the posse, Raphaël unties the ropes, tears the scarf off his face . . . off her face! He—

"Dinner is ready! Come wash your hands, Raphaël! At once!"

Five high towers, dozens of windows, a moat: this is the largest castle **ESTELLA** has ever built. She has drawn gardens around it. There are waterlily ponds with goldfish and swans; large ancient trees; wild rose and jasmine bushes; long alleys of pink gravel; lawns and brooks. The stone walls are covered with ivy, honeysuckle and vine. With a stick Estella draws the outer limit of her estate, stretching it further and further. She can enlarge it as she wishes. It is all sand, just sand, but she can see the lushness of the hedges and woods; she smells the wet grass, the lavender, the pines and cedar trees. Estella hears the birds and the song of the prince. Locked in a cell atop the keep, he awaits his punishment. He will be tortured, then put to death. Clenching a saw between her teeth, Estella scales the tower. She climbs all the way to the small window, gives the prince a quick kiss through the iron bars, saws them open, jumps into the cell. He embraces her. "Not now! The guards!" Estella swings her saw wildly (or is it a sword? Yes! A long shiny sword). She pokes one guard, cuts another one in half, stabs a third, a fourth, then a fifth one. "Jump!" she orders the prince. He hesitates. Estella pushes him through the window, slays another pair of guards and jumps in turn. They land atop two horses she had brought for their escape. Her cape flaps like a large flag.

A sudden gust of wind throws sand in Estella's eyes and mouth. Tumbleweeds rush across the road toward her. One wedges itself against the water tank; another leaps onto her castle, knocks down a few pebbles and bounces away toward Mr. Maxwell's house.

≈ ≈ ≈ ≈ ≈

D A Y

I N

S E P

T E M

B E R

16

Picture books are set in orderly rows throughout the apartment: in the office, in the library, in the living room. **RAPHAËL** is not allowed in his parents' bedroom but he knows this is where the largest stacks of magazines are kept. Sometimes he sneaks in and takes a few.

WorldAir. The comfort you deserve. Nonstop flights to Rio and Bangolore. The picture shows the cabin of an airplane. An elegant man is smiling at a pretty flight attendant who is smiling back at him, and so is the woman sitting next to him. They are all smiling, and elegant, and pretty. Raphaël's mother and father might be on this plane, going to Rio or Bangalore. Raphaël flips through the pages of the magazine. The sand is very white, like snow, and the water is turquoise blue. A woman lies on the beach, blond, long and lean. It is an advertisement for a deodorant or body lotion. The woman seems to enjoy herself tremendously. It must be the sun, the warmth and softness of the sand, the sizzle of the waves as they gently roll onto the shore. Raphaël knows he too would enjoy being there. Being with her, or being her. There are photographs of children, some older than him, some younger. A boy is drinking hot

cocoa, a girl is washing her hair. They all look happy.

Sometimes Raphaël leans over the balcony and looks at the children walking along the river. He tries to guess where they are going, whether they have brothers, sisters, a friend, a dog; whether they like movies and books and looking at magazines the way he does. He wonders if the woman walking beside them is their mother or Mademoiselle.

ᚱᚱᚱᚱᚱ

ESTELLA does not like recess. Having just joined this school, she feels excluded from the year-long friendships. In the classroom she blends in with the other children, but when she is in the yard she is left out. Some play ball, others play tag, two are comparing shoes and haircuts. Estella stands alone, walks a few steps toward one group, then toward another, never daring to come too close. If they feel that she is indeed too close, they stop playing or talking. They glance at her sideways, whisper and chuckle among themselves. Estella withdraws. She sits away from the others on the burning cement step, anxiously waiting for the bell to ring.

From a distance Estella watches a blond girl and a blond boy. They are sitting close together on

the low wall across the school yard. They are talking. Estella can't hear them but she can see their lips moving. They don't pay attention to her nor to anyone else. She can see them smile at each other. They look happy together. The blond boy unwraps a candy bar (it looks like chocolate) and offers some to the blond girl. Estella remembers the last time she had chocolate. A faint smile lights her face.

ᚱᚱᚱᚱᚱ

Weeks have passed. **RAPHAËL** can count the days on his calendar; he has crossed each one with a red pen. But it doesn't matter—the calendar is lying to him. Time remains still. Nothing ever seems to change. Day after day, the same duties, the same solitary games. The silence of his bedroom. And yet the warm air coming in through the open windows carries the new smell of leaves and blossoms. School will soon be over.

Joyful cries and laughter rise from the street. An endless stream of children walk the park daily. Many others have already left the city for summer vacation. Raphaël stares at the quail on his plate. He glances at his report card open on the dining room table, but he doesn't dare look up at his father and mother. It makes him feel uneasy to sit for dinner with his parents so unexpectedly.

A+ in history, A in geography. His other grades are average. "I don't want you to be merely average," his father tells him. He looks at Mademoiselle Rosamère with a quick, reproving stare, then at Raphaël's mother. "Raphaël will be taught English next year. This summer we should send him to an English boarding school or to a camp in America.

Raphaël sits on the same airplane he had seen in the magazine. But the flight attendant does not have time to smile at him much, and the woman sitting next to him does not smile at all. She might just be as worried as he is. "Beef or chicken?" asks the flight attendant. Raphaël doesn't answer. He can't speak. That would set free the tears that he tries to hold back.

It is a long flight from Paris to San Francisco.

A jet plane has drawn a thin white line across the sky. It is sharp and dazzling, then it broadens and fades softly, as a vanishing cloud. **ESTELLA** sits alone in the very back of the school bus.

23

Besides the driver, she is the only one left. For the last time she looks at the fields bordering the highway. They are dry and bare. All the tomatoes have been picked.

Today Estella talked to the blond girl and the blond boy. They didn't welcome her, but they didn't send her away, either. She introduced herself and they did too. She offered them a smile and they smiled back. Now Estella has to leave. She has to leave this school, Maxwell Ranch, the Mojave Desert. Her mother and her father need to find new jobs. They have to move on.

Estella's parents have heard of possible work in the North; they hope to be hired for the grape harvest in Napa Valley. Early in the morning the red pickup truck leaves Maxwell Ranch. The flatbed is loaded with furniture, boxes and trunks, leaving just enough space near the cabin for Estella to sit. Soon the wind will have erased the large eagle she has drawn on the sand. The old truck rattles along Highway 5, through the wide valley. Cultivated fields alternate with cattle ranches. The bright midday light gradually softens, coloring everything with rich yellow, orange and reddish tones. The purple shadows stretch more and more until they

cover all the land, drowning it in the deep blue haze of the evening. Only the very tops of the distant hills remain sunlit, as if a strand of liquid gold was flowing down their ridges.

Estella's heart is beating fast, and it hurts. She feels cold and she feels hot. A tear slides down her cheek, reaching her lip just as she smiles.

❧❧❧❧

On their way to the baseball park, the children from the summer camp are singing loudly, overjoyed to be taken to a Sunday game, a farewell field trip. **RAPHAËL** tries to sing along. He has learned some English these past two months.

Everything felt so different at first, so new. Home was so far away. Tomorrow he will be flying back to France, back to Paris and the large apartment on the river. Sitting on the bleachers with the other children, Raphaël now feels uncertain, as if floating in a dream. It is sunny. The field, a luminous green, is serene, soothing like a large pool of still water.

Estella's parents have worked hard, tending to the vines, then harvesting the grapes at the Gasparini Winery. As a reward Mr. Gasparini has offered them and Estella tickets to Sunday's baseball game. Estella sits between her mother and her father, waving a black and orange pennant. Not far from them, in a group of restless children, a boy is looking at her. The game has not yet begun. Players in crisp white uniforms run in pairs, throw balls back and forth, swing their bats, stretch on the grass.

The flags atop high masts dance in the light breeze. Raphaël looks at the stadium filling up fast, the hot dog and souvenir vendors, the players on the field. A small airplane flies by, pulling a streamer. He looks at the happy, noisy crowd. A girl is waving a flag. She stops and looks at him. Children have gathered near the dugout to try to get autographs from the players. As he walks down the stairs to join them, Raphaël turns back: the girl is gone.

Estella, a few steps back, follows the boy to the dugout. Maybe she too will get an autograph. Children push and shove. Holding out cards and baseballs, they call the names of their favorite players.

A tall baseball player turns around and slowly walks toward the children. He has noticed a quiet boy and a quiet girl. They don't hold any cards nor

DAY

IN

SEP

TEM

BER

any balls. They seem shy. The baseball player picks two balls off the ground and signs them. He gives one each to Estella and Raphaël. Pushed against the fence and against each other, they smile at him. A radiant, burning smile. They look at each other, their eyes sparkling.

Estella and Raphaël smile at each other.

For an instant, everything stops. The park is quiet and still. The children gathered around **ESTELLA & RAPHAËL** stare at them, motionless. The crowd and players are frozen, as in a photograph. The breeze drops, the flags sag. A seagull holds its flight, gently hovering high above the park. The light intensifies. Everything appears brighter. The sky is cobalt blue, vibrant and electric; the field, fluorescent; the dazzling uniforms glow as if lit from inside. The music, the cheers and laughter have died, replaced by a rich and deep silence.

Sitting at the Cactus Corners Café, an old and desolate crossroad coffeehouse, **RAPHAËL** flips through the pages of a newspaper that someone forgot. All month he has been traveling across the Mojave Desert, taking photographs for the photo agency he now works with in Paris. Suddenly he freezes, staring at the classified ads. So long ago …

He sits back, looks outside. Raphaël remembers coming to California as a boy. As he stares at the dry and bare landscape, he sees his own reflection in the window pane. He remembers summer camp. He remembers that warm day at the park. Raphaël looks tired and hasn't shaved, but his smile is the same.

Carrying her books and today's newspaper,

D A Y

I N

S E P

T E M

B E R

ESTELLA walks across the university campus. She is tall now. Her hair, which she used to wear shortly cropped as a young girl, reaches her waist. Having some time to spare before her history class, she lies down on the grass, away from the other students. Lying on her back, she looks at the clouds drifting by. She smiles. A warm beautiful smile. On the newspaper folded beside her, she has circled an ad in the personals section:

To: Girl and boy at ball game. **Warm day September. Years ago. Exchanged baseball for smiles. Call 916-756-7076.**

❧❧❧❧❧

Large trees line the quiet, narrow street. Golden spots of light dance on the shingled roofs, the pavement, the lawns. The sprinklers have stopped. A bluebird hops on the wet grass, searching for insects. The morning sun glistens through the leaves, sparkles on the rims of the two coffee cups, illuminates the photographs and souvenirs on the shelves. The signature on the old baseball bat has faded but one can still read the inscription: "To Estella and Raphaël." Resting against it, the framed newspaper clipping has turned to yellow and is spotted with mildew.

In the evening, when the sun is down and

D A Y

I N

S E P

T E M

B E R

the air is finally cooling off, Estella and Raphaël often walk to the lake, on the outskirts of town. As if it had captured the last warmth of the day, its smooth surface glows in the surrounding darkness. The night then turns the last shades of emerald, indigo and turquoise into one flat, solid black mass. As they return home Estella and Raphaël remain silent. They share the same thoughts.

ESTELLA & RAPHAËL often stay up late at night, telling their children tales of the Wild West and of Middle Age castles.

❧❧❧❧

31

Creative Editions is an imprint of The Creative Company, 123 South Broad Street, Mankato, Minnesota 56001.

Library of Congress

Cataloging-in-Publication Data

Nascimbene, Yan. A day in September/written and illustrated by Yan Nascimbene.

Summary: The lives of two isolated children, a wealthy young boy from Paris and the poor daughter of Mexican migrant workers, intersect at a baseball game in California with lasting results.

ISBN 0-15-200954-X   [1. Loneliness—Fiction.] I. Title.

PZ7.N1655Day 1995   [Fic]—dc20 94-45649

Printed in Italy   First edition   A B C D E

Designed by Rita Marshall